MELTING THE MASTER of MEAN

An Adventure in Kindness

ISBN: 978-1-4336-4575-4
Published by B&H Publishing Group Nashville, Tennessee
Unless otherwise noted, all Scripture references are taken from the
Holman Christian Standard Bible (HCSB).
Copyright © 1999, 2000, 2002, 2003, 2009 by Holman Bible Publishers,
Nashville, Tennessee. All rights reserved.
Printed in LongGang District, Shenzhen, China, June 2016
1 2 3 4 5 20 19 18 17 16

A car crashed into the Biblevan and was a total wreck. But the Biblevan fixed itself. Two brothers, Jimmy and Rupert, ran over to check on the Bibleteam.

Bibleman asked, "Where did the car's driver go?"

"There was no driver," Jimmy answered. "It drove itself!"

Jimmy's older brother spoke up. "Jimmy—you little twerp—didn't you see that creepy guy push the car down that hill?"

"Rupert, you big, fat liar—it drove itself!"

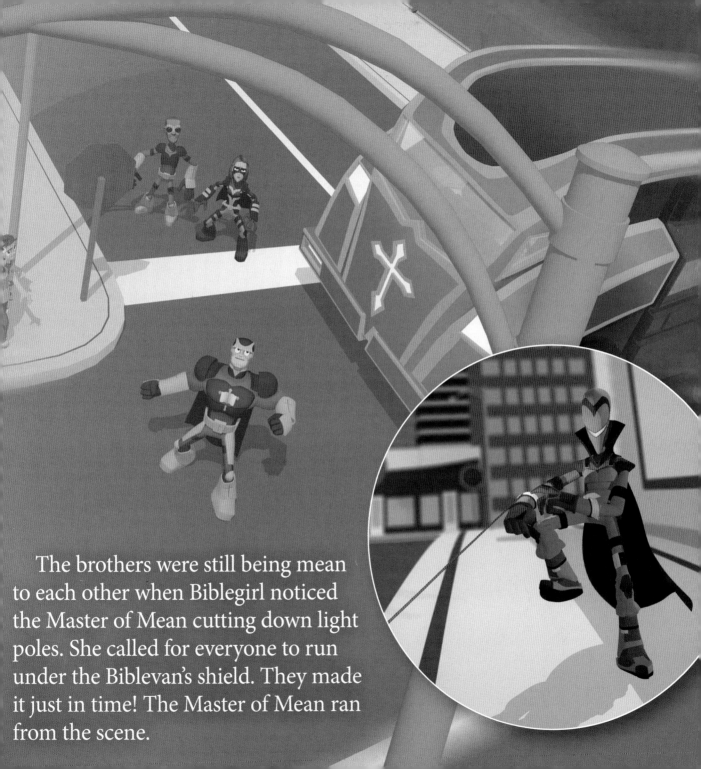

The brothers were still being mean to each other when Biblegirl noticed the Master of Mean cutting down light poles. She called for everyone to run under the Biblevan's shield. They made it just in time! The Master of Mean ran from the scene.

Biblegirl called the boys' father to come pick them up. While they waited, Bibleman talked to the boys, "The Master of Mean has made you very unkind. Rupert, here's a memory verse for you: Galatians 5:22 says, 'The fruit of the Spirit is kindness.'"

Cypher added, "Jimmy, your verse comes from Second Samuel 9:3. David had just become king and asked, 'Is there anyone left of Saul's family that I can show the kindness of God to?' You can just say, 'Is there anyone I can show the kindness of God to?'"

The boys' father picked them up, and then the Bibleteam went looking for the Master of Mean. Bibleman, Biblegirl, and Cypher had only driven a short distance when four empty cars all started moving toward them! Just before impact, the Biblevan blasted up into the air, and all four attacking vehicles crashed in a fiery collision.

Meanwhile, Melody spotted the Master of Mean from the Biblecopter; he was on top of the Baxter building.

Rupert and Jimmy had gone with their dad to his office. It was late in the afternoon, and people were going home.

"Good evening, Mr. Baxter," said someone walking past his open office door.

"Oh yes, George, good night," Mr. Baxter called back.

Little did he know what was happening on the roof of his own building.

The Master of Mean watched as the Biblevan drove right into his trap, and he launched a missile. Bibleman turned on the Biblevan's shield to deflect the missile up into the sky.

As the Biblevan pulled up in front of the Baxter building, Melody landed the Biblecopter nearby and ran toward the building.

Nobody in the corner office saw or heard the battle outside. Mr. Baxter was almost finished working, but he remembered the plants up on his rooftop garden still needed watering.

"We can do that, Dad," said Jimmy. "Rupert and I are practicing kindness today!" So the boys headed for the roof.

Meanwhile, down on the street, the Biblevan was surrounded by missile launchers as the Master of Mean watched from above. It wasn't safe for the Bibleteam to get out of the van.

Then several things happened at once:

Rupert and Jimmy entered the roof-top garden,

the Master of Mean ducked down to hide,

Melody started running up the stairs,

the Bibleteam saw their chance and got out of the van,

and Mr. Baxter finished his work and also headed for the roof.

Jimmy practiced his verse while watering plants. "Is there anyone I can show the kindness of God to? Second Samuel 9:3!"

The Master of Mean quietly gasped, "NO! Not KINDNESS! Not the Word of God! Arrrrgggghhh!"

Jimmy saw the man and moved toward him. "Excuse me, sir. Are you someone I can show the kindness of God to?"

The Master of Mean softly cried out, "Nooooo. . . !" He backed away from Jimmy. Just then, the Bibleteam reached the roof, and the villain's cape caught on one of his own missiles. Before he knew it, the missile launched, sending the Master of Mean flying off the roof and into the sky. "I'll get you for this Bibleman. I'll get you!"

Speaking and obeying God's Word defeated the enemy! Now Jimmy and Rupert not only know about the fruit of the Spirit from Galatians 5:22, they've witnessed the power of actually showing kindness to others.

The Mayor of Maybe may have caused doubt to grow in all those kids, but he couldn't snatch them out of the Father's hand.

When the gum landed, part of it stuck to one of the Biblecopter's turbines. Seeing this, Biblegirl quickly turned on the engine. The turbine began to inflate the wad of gum like a giant balloon. The Mayor got caught in the bubble! The Mayor realized his plan was failing. "I'll get you for this, Bibleman!" he said from inside the bubble. The gum blew away from the Biblecopter and rocketed into the sky.

As Emmanuelle spoke, the crate of bubble gum began to rumble and shake. The crate expanded and finally exploded—shooting a huge wad of liquid gum into the air!

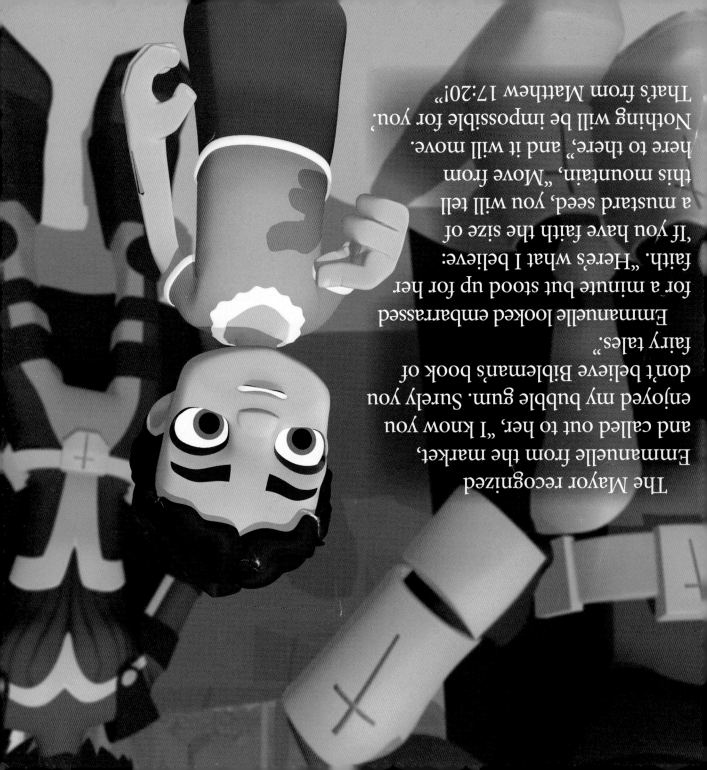

The Mayor recognized Emmanuelle from the market, and called out to her, "I know you enjoyed my bubble gum. Surely you don't believe Bibleman's book of fairy tales."

Emmanuelle looked embarrassed for a minute but stood up for her faith. "Here's what I believe: 'If you have faith the size of a mustard seed, you will tell this mountain, "Move from here to there," and it will move. Nothing will be impossible for you.' That's from Matthew 17:20!"

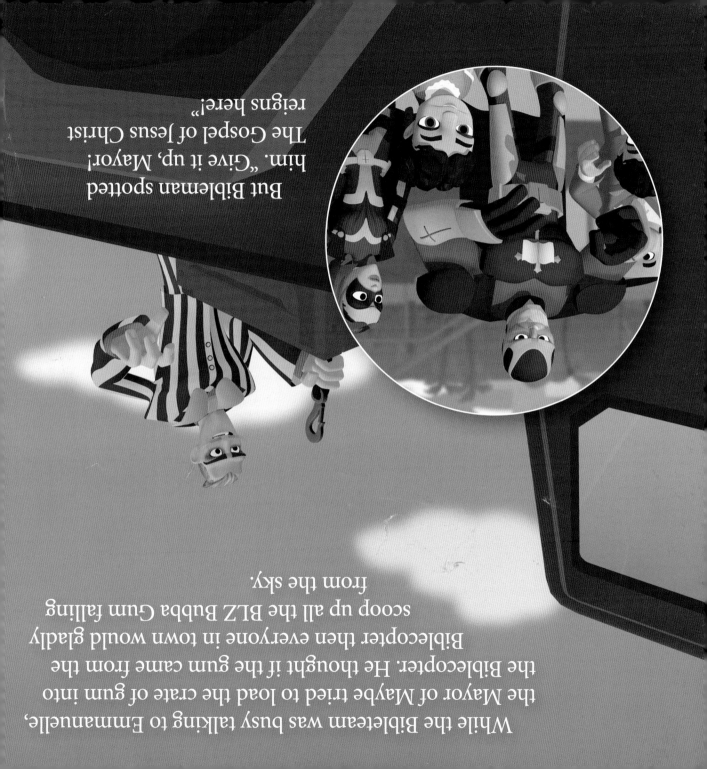

But Bibleman spotted him. "Give it up, Mayor! The Gospel of Jesus Christ reigns here!"

While the Bibleteam was busy talking to Emmanuelle, the Mayor of Maybe tried to load the crate of gum into the Biblecopter. He thought if the gum came from the Biblecopter then everyone in town would gladly scoop up all the BLZ Bubba Gum falling from the sky.

"Cypher's analysis said the more gum you eat, the more it attacks your faith."

Emmanuelle pulled all the wrappers out of her pocket, shocking everyone.

Faith knew just how to help her sister. "Emmanuelle, remember that our names together mean 'Believe God is with us.'" The twins hugged and prayed together. Emmanuelle confessed her doubt. She believed in Jesus!

Emmanuelle was not impressed with the story. Biblegirl was shocked. She didn't know what to do.

"How many pieces of bubble gum did you chew?" Bibleman asked.

"'Repent,' Peter said to them, 'and be baptized, each of you, in the name of Jesus Christ for the forgiveness of your sins, and you will receive the gift of the Holy Spirit.'"

Emmanuelle and her twin sister, Faith, were thrilled to meet Biblegirl. She told the girls about the first Gospel sermon ever preached in the second chapter of Acts: "Peter preached to the Jews in Jerusalem just a few days after Jesus went back to heaven, telling them about Jesus' sacrifice and gift of forgiveness.

Bibleman turned to the pastor. "I want to take this crate back to HQ for disposal. Can you help me get it to the Biblecopter?"

Pastor Deveaux replied, "Yes, of course. But I wonder, could you help young Emmanuelle, a girl who has been deeply affected by this bubblegum?"

"We would love to," said Bibleman.

The Mayor of Maybe kept an eye on his precious cargo. "Perhaps this will work out for me after all. Why not use the helicopter to distribute my bubble gum?"

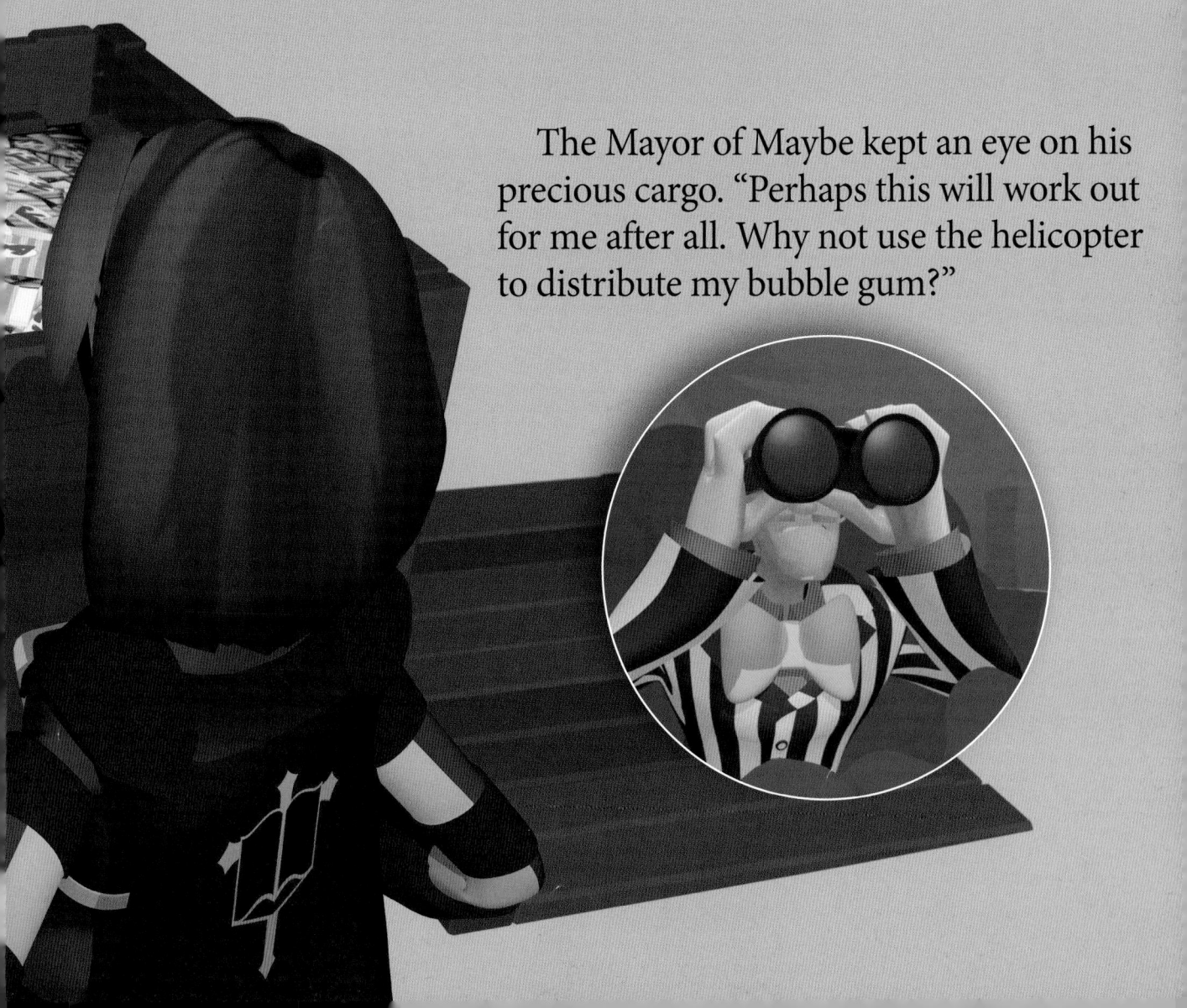

Bibleman and Biblegirl found a crate that was filled with thousands of pieces of BLZ Bubba Gum. "We need to test this gum to find out exactly what we're dealing with," Biblegirl said. "I'll send a scan to Cypher at HQ."

Pastor Deveaux called Bibleman, who quickly flew down with Biblegirl. The Bibleteam soon identified the evil villain.

"Pastor, we're dealing with the Mayor of Maybe," said Bibleman.

Biblegirl explained, "The Mayor of Maybe uses different schemes, but his goal is always to make kids doubt their faith in the Gospel of Jesus Christ. Let's go take some scanner readings."

Pastor Deveaux went to the local market to find the source of the bubble gum. There he saw a man in a booth giving out the free candy to all the kids. Then a bus passed in front of him, blocking the pastor's view. When the bus pulled away, the man and his booth were gone! All that was left was a gum wrapper.

Emmanuelle just shrugged and
popped a bubble from the gum she was chewing. The pastor
looked around and was stunned to see many more children refusing to
walk into church, and they were all chewing bubble gum!

"I have never seen these children chew bubble gum before," he thought
to himself. "What is happening here?"

One Sunday morning Pastor Deveaux saw a young girl arguing with her parents: "No! I don't want to go to church. You can't make me!"

The pastor asked her, "Emmanuelle, why are you saying that?"

BIBLEMAN®
THE ANIMATED ADVENTURES

THE MAYOR OF MAYBE DOLES OUT DOUBT

An Adventure with the Gospel